5

Christopher Browne

STRONG AS STONE

VIKING

Stone lived in a tiny village
surrounded by giant mountains.

She lived among her family and friends
and the bison and elk and mastodons.

While the village kids played hop-skull,
Stone spent time with her dad.
He taught her everything he knew.

Stone learned
to be brave
and strong,

fierce

and kind.

When she was hurt or scared, her dad would whisper, "You may not know it yet, but you are as strong as stone."

It was a good life.
Until Stone's dad became sick.
The village elders knew of only one
cure, found deep within the mountains.

But a willing warrior would have to make it
past the ferocious bears guarding the cure.
And there were none willing.
It was just too dangerous.

So Stone volunteered.
She knew she was strong enough.
Her dad had told her so.

The mountains were dark—
and cold.

Stone felt
small and alone.

Stone was about to have
her first meal in days, when
a beast dropped in for a bite.

She roared and acted
as fierce as possible . . .

Which didn't feel right.

Stone took pity on the beast and whispered,
"You may not know it yet, but you are as
strong as stone."

She taught the beast
everything she knew.

The journey
wasn't easy.

The mountains were still dark and cold. But Stone no longer felt small and alone.

Which helped when the ferocious
bears emerged from the shadows.

Stone had grown up hearing stories of
the warriors who left to fight the bears.
The warriors were brave, strong, and fierce.

But there was one thing
the warriors were not . . .

The warriors were not kind.

Kindness made Stone stronger than any warrior who had come before her.

And it made her as strong as stone.

Stone returned to her tiny village
surrounded by giant mountains.

She returned to her family and friends
and the bison and elk and mastodons.

But most importantly,
Stone returned to her dad.

And Dad
returned
to Stone.

To my
FIERCE LITTLE LADY HARRIET

VIKING

An imprint of Penguin Random House LLC, New York

First published in the United States of America by Viking,

an imprint of Penguin Random House LLC, 2021

Viking & colophon are registered trademarks

of Penguin Random House LLC.

Visit us online at penguinrandomhouse.com

LIBRARY OF CONGRESS CATALOGING-IN-PUBLICATION DATA IS AVAILABLE

ISBN 9780593204665

Manufactured in China   Book design by Jim Hoover   Typeset in Le Havre Rough and Steam

The illustrations in this book were created both digitally as well as by hand using pencil, charcoal, and watercolor.

1   3   5   7   9   10   8   6   4   2